WestBow Press books may be ordered through booksellers or by contacting:

WestBow Press
A Division of Thomas Nelson
1663 Liberty Drive
Bloomington, IN 47403
www.westbowpress.com
1-(866) 928-1240

ISBN: 978-1-4497-9022-6 (sc)
ISBN: 978-1-4908-0836-9 (e)

Library of Congress Control Number: 2013905973

Printed in the United States of America.

WestBow Press rev. date: 09/23/2013

California Stories of Pickers, Builders, and Healers

Anna Marie Hernandez

WestBow
PRESS
A DIVISION OF THOMAS NELSON

DEDICATION

*To all the pickers, builders, and healers of California
who enriched all of our lives.*

TABLE OF CONTENTS

ILLUSTRATIONS

Prologue

California Stories of Pickers, Builders, and Healers is an assortment of biographical stories that took place in a rural desert town. The chronology of the town spans from the early 1920's to the present time. This book was written to preserve the flavor and essence of an old railroad town, known to Hollywood celebrities of the 1930's, and once home to Native American tribes, and later home to Roy Rogers and Dale Evans.

The stories describe uniquely colorful individuals who were pickers, builders, and healers. Each of these individuals left an indelible stamp of service and compassion, which preserved the community for future generations. It has been my intent to honor their contributions in these stories and to help preserve the memory of a once vibrant, fascinating California town.

Music of the Town

In an old town where the wind whispered at night to cottonwoods and songs slowly faded into dreams, church bells rang from an old mission church. The church had a very high steeple. It was surrounded by towering fir trees where hundreds of birds chirped all day, when the church bells rang.

From the steeple, church bells rang every hour of the day and at noon for the midday Angelus prayer. The church bells could be heard as far as the river that flowed under the cottonwoods, past the park and train depot. It was to this old mission church, that I came often as a child with Grandpa.

It all began in the choir loft, one Sunday morning in early May. Monsignor Van, the old Belgian parish priest, had just started Mass when suddenly the church walls resonated. The church lamps hanging from the rafters swayed. All the twittering birds outside paused with great expectations to listen.

Up on the choir loft, a choir sang the songs of angels. Heavenly music filled the church. The choir swayed to and fro with the church lamps like swinging pendulums. The former Broadway director's arms swirled in midair. He punctuated the musical refrains as if he were still directing the old Broadway musicals in New York City.

Grandpa sniffled and cried tears of joy. He murmured, "I hear a choir of angels."

door, we could still smell wet sawdust on the floor. In the shadows of time, we heard a butcher hum as he sliced the meat.

"Do you remember," began Grandpa, "the meat we bought for tamales?" The butcher hummed as he pounded the meat. He hummed louder as he wrapped it in crinkly butcher paper as he filled the customers' orders. He hummed loudest as he rang up the cash register. His humming filled our ears.

The church bells called us to the park. Scraggly elm trees shaded an abandoned bandstand with a dance floor.

"Do you remember the church fiestas?" asked Grandpa. Grandpa and Papa would build a booth with a narrow screen door in the center of the park. From that central booth, pots of Grandmother's tamales were sold for all the church fiestas.

"I remember the music," I replied vaguely. The townspeople danced through the starry night, while musicians played on the bandstand. My cousins and I devoured lime snow cones and mounds of cotton candy. The laughter of children playing and neighbors sharing on park tables were the best music of the church fiestas.

The train depot stood at the edge of the park. It had a wood squeaky floor. Inside the depot had sat a bespectacled, squinting telegraph operator. He was a wiry man with the seriousness of the town mortician. His words were sparse, but his fingers were nimble. He cranked out countless telegraphs across the country.

"Do you remember," began Grandpa, "all the telegrams we sent?" I nodded again. I remembered the clanging of the telegraph. It had a musical sound uniquely peculiar.

Across the train depot flowed a crooked stream. Grandpa and I walked to the bubbling stream that had been a wide river that swooshed by the town.

"Do you remember the sound of the river that watered my fruit trees?" asked Grandpa.

"I remember slimy tadpoles and squishy sand between my toes," I replied.

The church bells began to ring for the midday Angelus prayer just as the old Santa Fe train sounded its whistle. The branches of the old cottonwoods formed a steeple over our heads, as we listened to the ringing bells and the whistling train.

Wiping his eyes, Grandpa lamented, "Soon my child, all these places will be gone. Nobody will remember anything ever again." The wind whispered mournfully through the bent cottonwoods.

The church bells were ringing for Mass one early Sunday morning when Grandpa was called to a heavenly home. He often talked about going to a place where choirs of angels sang day and night. At least, he would hear inspired music and be free to pick any fruit he wanted where he was going.

Many decades transpired and much of Old Town was a distant memory just as Grandpa had predicted. Then, the unexpected happened.

Square, brown metal signs appeared in odd places to mark "historical" places in town. They appeared by order of the Mayor, before vacant lots and deserted alleys. One sign marked the cemetery and another marked the old river. There even appeared a square sign by the mission church where the bells had once rung.

Soon after, tourists pursued square signs everywhere in town. They carried maps that described the old places. As I walked around Old Town, I heard them talk. They argued and debated among themselves as if they were the old timers instead of passing tourists.

"The sign says there was a park with a bandstand and dance floor."

"Can you believe that there was a train depot with a telegraph operator?"

"How can one baker bake for an entire town?"

"Is it true that there were apple trees and family owned orchards here?"

Such occurrences were hard for the uninformed to imagine, much less to even believe.

"Yes, it used to be that way," I finally replied one day to some skeptical tourists. "Music filled this town from the old mission church to the train depot." However, they only scoffed at me as they stared at the weed-filled lots and many thrift stores along the main street.

Then, I remembered that Sunday morning when once there had sung a choir of angels that had made the church lamps sway, the twittering birds pause to listen, and Grandpa walk to remember. Music had filled the entire town. Its echoes still remained for anyone who cared to listen. I promised to remember as long as the wind whispered at night to the old cottonwoods and songs slowly faded into dreams.

Grandma

Grandma's kitchen window overlooked the entire world. Before the window a vast Californian desert unfolded itself for miles. In the distance a few cottonwoods lined the Mohave River alongside railroad tracks. Across the tracks was another world altogether. The river was on this side of the tracks, and at night we could hear the crickets and river sounds when not interrupted by the train.

The tracks separated the town. The train was not an invasion to us, but it had a song of its own, a steady flowing rhythm. From the crooked screen door to the unpaved roads this side of the tracks, the train was just as much a part of life as the morning crowing when the roosters woke us.

At the window we counted train cars. Grandma and I counted out loud. We numbered each car until the train disappeared grumbling under the bridge. Grandma's eyes, roving and alert, would travel beyond the cottonwoods and passing trains. She was forever tracing the outlines of the hills popping into the blue horizon. Perhaps, she remembered former days working in the grape fields of California during the summer months.

Working in the fields was hard work. As the afternoon progressed, the temperatures rose over one hundred degrees. The sand was hot, but she would work each row alongside the men. Rising at three-thirty in the morning to wash clothes and retiring late from the grape fields, Grandma often sang according to the neighbors. She still had to return home to prepare supper for a large family. Exhausted, she would fall asleep while singing and nursing her youngest son. Whatever she sang blessed her with physical endurance. If the entire family worked hard during the summer, there would be sacks of flour, rice, and beans for the entire winter. Grandma would have food in her basement pantry all year.

Perhaps, the passing train spinning through the desert hills reminded Grandma of other scenes and places. Irrespective of her thoughts, Grandma would abandon the kitchen window sighing as the train vanished.

The kitchen was Grandma's inner world of reality. No one dared to enter or leave the kitchen without sitting down at the table. So it happened, all pleasure and business had their humble origin in the kitchen. Grandma was a champion tortilla maker. Her many sons boasted of the picnic tortillas made of scrambled eggs, beans and chili that she would make for their lunches. At the table I used to sit, hand on chin, watching her make tortillas that formed and collapsed, squeaking under her dish cloth. For some odd reason, I half hoped to see a busted tortilla. However, it never did happen.

A rare aroma of chili grounded with vanilla penetrated to the core of the kitchen. In the black metate glistened garden chili while nearby a scrubbed face coffee pot gurgled and bubbled over the stove. Pushed against the wall on the table reposed the fat sugar bowl. Off to the side counter loomed his rival, the cookie box. Inside were the coveted fig cookies.

At the end of the kitchen starched curtains rustled, drawing late afternoon silhouettes on the linoleum floor, and just above the sink a round clock ticked the hours away. That funny clock always pouted at me for leaving blue bowls in the sink. By no means were these ordinary bowls. Drinking lentil soup from these royal bowls transformed lunch. Mealtime became a banquet. Spooning soup was a delight. I would hurry to scrape the bowl's sides to unearth the bottom. Underneath were the loveliest blue milkmaid and the skinniest apple tree ever painted.

Not too far from the kitchen, the yellow canary often meditated upside down. The bird could have been engaged in a yoga rite. Nevertheless, from his trance the bird would awaken at the sound of the train. Winding up a few chirps, he would fluff out his feathers and explode into an intense, passionate song. The canary sang in beautiful Spanish according to Grandmother. She said, "My canary makes lots of birds sing." What animated stories the kitchen told to the open heart.

Outside, the gray alley cat paraded meowing off key. Inside, Grandma ignored him pounding tortillas in a rhythm Bach couldn't dispute. There was no sweeter sound in all the earth than kitchen music. Its simplicity instilled a trust in me for the goodness of life.

Grandma had a secret way of instilling courage. It was one spring morning that I ran to the house panting and flung the dented screen door open. To a six-year-old imagination, being chased by the family dog was no less than fleeing from the jungle boar. Wiser than a century old scholar, Grandma peered at me over spectacles and laughed. After hearing my tale, she gathered a few crackers and headed to the door. "Lady" trotted meekly behind us to the corral. My grandmother's intuitive common sense christened fear into strength.

One late Saturday, Grandma was engrossed over a little envelope. She guarded her envelope. With trembling hands she traced a letter with the pencil. Copying the letters of her name onto a church envelope was a painful task. She smiled sheepishly at me. My grandmother never had occasion to write her own name.

The years stole by. Gone were the mornings she and I could walk two streets down to the corner grocery store. Her hands no longer braided my unruly hair, and crocheted dish clothes remained undone. Tartly crisp, the day before Christmas Eve, a violent storm raged outside the hospital windows. As the winter winds whipped around the buildings, we stood hushed before Grandma's bed. I held her hand for the last time. She did not open her eyes. As the winds howled, far away there came other images. In Grandma's bedroom stood a sad, tiny girl peering into a silent bird cage and crying, "He's dead."

"He's not dead," said Grandma with finality. "The canary went home." As my grandmother gasped for air and a hush filled the hospital room, I understood suffering. I realized what it meant to love. In the grape fields and at home, through bad times and good times, amid tears and laughter, Grandma had triumphed. Leaving the hospital room, I heard the canary. He was singing softly that storm-rent afternoon Grandma was called home.

Watching the flaming red of the winter sky a few weeks later before my thirteenth birthday, my cousin and I sat on the front lawn, by the lamp post. In the distance I heard an old echo. It was a familiar sound.

It barged inward like a thousand ringing chimes of happy memories. Ears perked, I listened. From behind the rolling hills thundered the train, whistle shrilling. Leaping up, I tore down the slope into the desert.

"Where are you going?" demanded my startled cousin.

"To count train cars," I shouted over my shoulder pointing to the hills.

"You can't see the train," she shouted back.

"I can hear it," I yelled bounding forward. I stopped on a mound of dirt listening and wistfully counting to the sinking sun.

On tiptoes before the kitchen window waiting, an afternoon sun emanates off Grandma's happy face. However, Grandma does not care. She is much too busy counting train cars with a little girl.

The Revelation

He was concealed against the church hall wall. It was his first Sunday at his newly assigned parish. The reserved Italian priest, with piercing blue eyes, nervously fidgeted. The parish hall was empty, except for a few gray-haired grandmothers with their pesky grandchildren. They ate all the reception cake, oblivious to the discomfort of their new parish priest.

A reception to welcome the new priest from Argentina had been announced from the pulpit, but few parishioners had bothered to stop by. The children had run ahead to the hall for their portion of the reception cake. He fidgeted uncomfortably against the wall. The reception was for him, but there was no one to greet him. As I entered the empty hall, I quickly sought him out. He ventured forward reluctantly. Quietly he asked, "Are you looking for me?"

There was no smile, no greeting, only resigned sadness in his eyes. He looked briefly at me, and then looked away. His glance combed the overgrown trees in the courtyard to the distant hills. I surmised then and there, that the austere Bishop had assigned this young man the job no priest ever wanted. It was an immigrant mission church, already in its eighty-sixth year, in a rural town. It was situated in the old part of town which was now gang and drug infested. The church buildings were emaciated with time and abuse. Graffiti adorned the back walls of the church. Massive cracks lined the exterior church walls. Rain leaked in on the back wall behind the altar, while darkness prevailed within the church. No priest had taken the initiative to refurbish any part of the church in over fifty years.

His eyes sorrowfully gazed into the distance. This present assignment was his banishment from civilization. In the dancing summer sunlight, which poured through the open door, I caught a greenish hue around the rim of his haunting blue eyes. It was his profound resignation that captured my attention. After mumbling a few words of welcome and cursory introductions, I left him in the middle of the parish hall. At least he was detached from the wall for others to welcome him.

Over the course of the next several weeks, I was to learn much about this young trilingual priest. He had come to this country speaking only Spanish and entered the seminary twenty-two years prior. He had already served fifteen years as a priest in one of the largest regional dioceses. Since his Argentinean Spanish was more articulate than that of the California natives, he had been assigned to poor parishes with church schools.

This was his first assignment without the responsibility of a parish school. He made clear from day one that he missed not interacting with young school children. It was a harsh assignment, given that there were no assistant priests assigned to help him. He was relegated to celebrate six Masses and hear confessions every weekend, regardless of his state of health or any personal pastoral desire.

The fit young priest was a runner by true ambition. Running was his passion, his hobby, and his personal release from the sorrows that he carried. In his detachment from the world, I detected a searing soul pain that could never be placated by anyone, anything, or any pastoral assignment.

Whatever heavy resignation he carried, he compensated with a zeal for numerous building projects. He was a builder priest, and true to his Italian name, his personal stamp of zeal would enter every building project. In his last parish assignment, he had beautified the church with a courtyard complete with fountains and shade trees. It was his passion for building with his hands that distinguished him from other priests who contented themselves with only preaching every Sunday.

Within a few weeks the repairs had begun without any announcement. The sign of the new pastoral direction began without formal discussion or parish council consent. If ever there were miraculous staircases built, there would be more marvels to attest to the ingenuity of this foreign-born priest.

It was one late August, in the blistering desert heat that construction began on the roof of the adjacent vacant cottage. The cottage had been lived in for many years, by a recluse, who had the ironic fortune of having the last name which meant "cubbyhole" in Spanish. Some would argue that this three room structure was only a storage cubbyhole which didn't merit any renovation. The entire project entailed a new house roof, exterior and interior paint, and extending the cement patio. The cypress trees were discarded and grown apricot and apple trees were planted alongside dozens of magnificent rose bushes.

It seemed a misfortune that the caretaker who had lived so long in this house had not lived long enough to witness the transformation. Señora Casillas had a penchant for decorating the altar with any wild flower or long weed that grew in her untidy yard. She had lived rent-free, in the church cubbyhole, in return for cleaning candles and beautifying the church. The old Spanish-speaking lady soon became the eyes and ears of every successive pastor.

As Señora Casillas sat on her front porch, she observed the coming and going of all parishioners who entered and left the sanctuary. She roamed the inside church picking up debris or chasing boisterous children outdoors. She was an old woman without a family. Her adopted family was the church. Like a devoted mother, Señora Casillas saw and heard everything. She saw priests energetically enter and gladly retire from the church. She witnessed countless baptisms, marriages, and burials. Over the years many drifted away, and only a few faithful remained to support the mission church.

Deceased well over twenty years, now only the old woman's devoted spirit permeated the holy grounds as the workers toiled on the roof and dug up a broken irrigation system. It was on that blistering August Saturday, as I hurried to the vigil Mass, that I heard the Mexican workers complain about the new priest. They grumbled, "This new priest gets impatient. He wants everything done overnight."

It would be the mantra for this church. Miraculous marvels would be done at lightning speed, as he paced the sidewalk, like a restless lion overseeing the building projects. He was not beyond digging a few ditches himself, or carrying heavy pipes to speed the progress of the workers.

It was thus the debate arose, within the parishioners, as to the nature of this particular project that totally consumed the attention of the priest. It was as if Señora Casillas had returned herself again, to spur the new priest forward, to beautify her old haunting grounds. Some parishioners contended that certainly this cubbyhole was destined to be the future home for the new priest.

Others argued it would be home to any hapless assistant assigned to this wayward town of gangs, homeless, and eccentric derelicts. Others put forth the argument that this cubbyhole was only a storage closet for cleaning supplies and tools of that sort. However, the confessionals had been relegated to that unholy usage, since the few faithful had long abandoned the sacrament of reconciliation.

It was curiosity about the first building project that attracted crowds of observers who offered their diverse opinions. It was certainly fodder for Sunday discussion, especially when the roses were planted and the irrigation system repaired. After the young priest hung a huge hammock on the front porch, it was a matter of consensus. It had to be the home for the newly arrived priest. It was a marvel to behold. The roof had been installed atop a mustard-yellow painted house. Wood flooring was laid and the windows were meticulously tinted blue. The patio courtyard extended almost to the back alley, adding a new dimension to the renovated cottage.

If Señora Casillas had returned, she would have been well-pleased with the efforts of the young priest, all except for the tinted windows. She had spent her time watching others, unlike this priest, who was watched intensely by others. The priest valued his privacy, whereas, the last owner had become part of the church landscape. It was the opinion of the congregation, that the pastor had chosen the last caretaker's house for his new quarters. The cubbyhole had been transformed into a delightful summer cottage.

Opposite the cottage, other renovations appeared, visible through the windows on the second floor of the rectory. A floral sofa materialized, alongside a bedside lamp, across a large plasma television set. A decorative mantle mirror adorned the wall facing the street. It reflected the world at large, without the priest ever having to look out the French double doors, which opened over a wide balcony. I argued that the cubbyhole could not be the new pastoral residence. Yet the consensus prevailed. No one would renovate a house that did not serve some utilitarian purpose or ministerial function. The priest dutifully parked his gray truck every day in the driveway. He came and went often through the cottage front door.

The verdict was given despite my best arguments with fellow parishioners. The old caretaker's house was the new priest's official residence.

The answer to the strange enigma came six months later, after the completion of the handicap access into the church. I had come unusually early, for the vigil Mass, to escape the gloom of the dreary winter day. I welcomed the solitude of the inner sanctuary. It was the custom of the Italian priest to play a tape of Gregorian chants before the vigil Mass began. As the fading afternoon light poured through the stained glass windows, igniting the church in hues of medieval colors, I fancied myself in an old monastery of Cistercian monks.

As I approached the church steps, I saw him exit. He emerged from the front door of the cottage cradling a long bundle, tucked mysteriously under his arms. I bounded forward to greet him. He noticed me and quickened his pace. As he darted past the front door, I called his name.

Quickly, he stuffed his mysterious bundle further into his black jacket. His cheeks were reddened by the winter wind that had begun to blow. He kept walking, as if I were only an apparition, brought forth by the changing season. He was in no mood for social exchange of any sort.

It was then, that I noticed his bundle move. A slender tail wagged. He finally turned, irritated by my earthly female intrusion, upon his priestly thoughts. As I approached, I saw a scraggly beagle with restless eyes that matched the temperament of its owner. He pressed the dog like a newborn babe into his muscular chest. This creature was his loyal companion, trusted friend, and solitary playmate.

As I moved toward him, he retreated from me, visibly annoyed. I had stumbled upon his cherished secret. He was a new priest with a street dog. It appeared to have no particular breeding or training. Of the many priests I had ever known, none had I encountered, with a house dog that demanded any priestly attention.

Irritably, he pushed the dog further into his jacket, as I innocently asked about its gender. "It's female," he retorted, punctuating the words, as he hurried into his rectory.

I pondered the dilemma of the young priest with his secret female companion. Had the church coffers been poured into the first building project for a street dog? I reasoned that the dog had to be a most trusted companion for a priest banished to a remote desert town.

A few weeks later, after the first winter snow, I was again leaving church, when I was enlightened about the true occupant of the refurbished cottage. At the end of Mass, the priest had admonished us not to exit the side door. The adjacent sidewalk was frosted with ice. His stern admonishment was my open invitation. I had already noticed the light in the middle room of the cottage. The revelation was at now hand. Quickly, I exited the side door. As careful as I was not to fall, a young kid with a mop of black hair slid past me smoothly across the icy sidewalk.

Slightly unnerved, I clutched the hand rail feeling extremely foolish, as I peered across to the old caretaker's cottage. A floor lamp illuminated the room. There on the sofa, on a well-worn quilt, under the light she reposed. The beagle awaited the arrival of her beloved master. An inviting warmth permeated the room. There was a timeless bond between a faithful dog and its owner. A well-loved beagle deserved a house of her own, complete with fruit trees and fragrant roses. Señora Casillas would have been pleased indeed. She was still looking out her window watching over this young Italian priest and his renovated church.

Several months later, after having observed the enigmatic priest walking his dog along the street, I bravely ventured another furtive meeting with him. As he expanded on his building marvels, I had enthusiastically captured every masterpiece with my camera. The church had new stucco and had been painted in earth tones. The interior church was well-lit, and the graffiti-filled walls facing the alley torn down. The fruit trees had yielded the first summer fruit. The roses perfumed the hot August evening with their fragrance. I clutched my photos of the church and its courtyards. There were pictures of the cottage and even a panoramic view of the church from the street.

Nervously, I cradled my work of art. I took my place against the church wall, among the many parishioners who assembled after Mass, to talk with the priest. He stood at the front door speaking with a prospective donor. She completely engaged his attention with her animated conversation.

In his zeal for another donor, he ignored the rest of us. The sacristan's wife soon grew tired and turned her walker around to sit. She fanned herself impatiently in front of him.

The Filipino choir director paced behind, with a statue for the priest to bless, while the sacristan paced in front. I fidgeted with my photos against the cool stucco wall.

After what seemed an eternal wait at the pearly gates of heaven, the priest finally turned his attention to us. Dutifully, he blessed the statue held by the choir director, and he answered the sacristan's questions. It took all my courage to disengage myself from the church wall.

He thumbed through the photographs indifferently without comment. I attempted vainly to draw his attention to his building masterpieces. Once again he turned to gaze sorrowfully into the distance. It was the same sorrowful expression in his blue eyes when I first welcomed him. My second meeting with him had provoked yet another sorrow.

"Are these for me?" he asked with resignation. I nodded. Quietly, he tucked the photos back into the envelope and turned his attention to the remaining parishioners demanding his attention. I had been dismissed quickly again. Rebuffed, I tried to find comfort in my distorted reasoning. Perhaps, this enigmatic priest had been destined to oversee great cathedrals instead of renovating old mission churches. Could it be that he dreamed of the faithful flocking to this mission church and filling its coffers? Whatever the reason for the priest's sorrow, I would never know. As a few parishioners gathered around the priest, he seemed strangely at home. He had found another flock in a distant California desert.

When I gazed at the caretaker's cottage, I saw the old woman sitting on her porch curiously watching me. She had seen it all. Señora Casillas had seen my photographs and heard every word. The beagle peered out the front door. The dog waited anxiously for her master, and Señora Casillas waited for another time, when the faithful would return once more.

The Clouds Are Changing Colors

Panpipe music drifted across the bedroom from the tape recorder. Dad sat in his hospital bed rolling and knotting up the bed sheets. For over twenty years, he had been a teacher and school principal. Parkinson's disease had taken its toll. No longer able to sit by himself or eat solid food, Dad kept himself busy tying and untying bed sheets all day across the bed rails. It was part of his builder instinct.

Outside, dove-shaped clouds bobbed through the summer sky. The clouds were tinged with streaks of gray. Shifting restlessly in bed, Dad turned to me and asked, "How long will it take me to die?"

The last strains of panpipe music floated across the room as I wept for him. I prayed for a sign from heaven. Dad reached for my hand and gently massaged my arm. "You won't hurt now," he murmured closing his eyes. The clouds had turned charcoal-gray. *Outside, the clouds were changing colors. They were passing through the silent night.*

When I was small, Dad used to wake me before dawn.

"Come look at the sky," he would call to me.

"I'm afraid," I complained. "It's dark and cold outside."

As we stood outside shivering under the bright stars, Dad would point to the clouds in the sky. "Don't be afraid," he admonished. *"The clouds are changing colors. They are passing through the night."*

20

There were clouds for every season. There were magical clouds to laugh under and ominous clouds to weep by. There were clouds filled with surprises and clouds to dream by in the gates of time.

As Dad watched the clouds tossed high in the sky, breaking into colors he spoke to me about the past. In the spring, we chased cottontails beneath aqua-soaked clouds. In the summer, we ran through fields after pearl-white clouds. When autumn arrived, we kicked leaves under burnt-orange clouds. As winter descended, we pranced through the snow as misty clouds tumbled across the sky. These were our shared memories never to be forgotten.

When the relatives arrived to visit Dad, they kept their distance from him. Dad pointed to the sky and hoarsely spoke. "My dad is crossing through the port. I am going home soon."

When the relatives heard Dad talk about Grandpa, they left the room in a hurry without even saying goodbye. Even though they did not see beyond the room, in the clouds, I saw images of Grandpa and heard echoes of the past.

Through the windows of time, I saw Dad stringing Christmas lights around the nativity scene as I played the piano for Grandpa. One Christmas Eve, a tape recorder hidden behind the nativity scene, played my piano music for the entire world to hear. *"Silent Night! Holy Night! All is calm, All is bright."*

Dad was renowned for his handcrafted outdoor Christmas decorations of camels, sheep, shepherds, and the Wise Men. Every year he built a new addition and added it to an expansive outdoor nativity crèche. When he wasn't engaged helping to build another family park or school library in the community, he busied himself at home with countless building projects. Dad had built an office, a backyard grape arbor, a shrine with a fountain, and several sheds for his many building tools. During the course of his lifetime, he had built several spare rooms, tables, bookcases, and other functional devices. He was not beyond coming to the assistance of others for helping them with their personal building projects.

Father gestured impatiently to the clouds forming in the sky. The clouds were fiery magenta. *The clouds were changing colors. They were passing through the silent night.*

The neighbors also came to visit bringing stuffed animals which Dad hurled across the room. The neighbors hurriedly left shaking their heads. They failed to hear the clouds weeping. The clouds were pearly white. *The clouds were changing colors. They were passing through the silent night.*

As Dad neared the end of his journey, we spent more time together watching the sky. As the clouds chased each other skipping across the sky, they changed into windmills. Dad listened as I reminisced about family vacations.

One late summer night as we returned from a trip, Dad pulled the 1956 station wagon over into the grape fields. He could not find any lodging in town for our family. There was no room in the inn for us. The night was silent in the grape fields. The night was bright under the stars. The night was calm as we slept under the grapevines until the field workers woke us in the morning.

The clouds were glimmering turquoise. *The clouds were changing colors. They were passing through the silent night.*

Changing Clouds

The last week as Dad slipped into a coma, a gray-headed gentleman came to visit. An angel in disguise, this man came with a rosebud in his hand and a story in his heart.

"Long ago when your dad was a boy," he began, "he was a track star. He ran to win the state finals at the coliseum. On the day of the great race, your dad was far behind the front runner. It didn't look like he was going to win, but something from within spurred him on. He came from behind and won the race at the coliseum."

The stately looking gentleman smiled as he remembered. "He held that record for thirty years." Placing the rosebud on Dad's pillow, he whispered to him, "For your final race, sir."

There were no silver medals to hold. There were no newspaper clips to show. There was only a familiar story to tell. The clouds were sailing through the timeless sky like vast silver barges. *The clouds were changing colors. They were passing through the silent night,* as I waited for my sign.

It was a cool summer night, when the panpipe music awoke me past midnight. Three tall vigil candles were burning, scenting the room with incense. As Mother combed Dad's hair, she said, "Now you are ready." Dad was sweating and breathing heavily with his chest and face. In his right hand he squeezed a small, furry lamb.

By the candles' flickering light in the cool breeze, Mother and I sat and watched. From the tape recorder, panpipe music played. Above the flute music, memories from the past sounded from the walls. We heard distant voices of laughter and pain. We felt joy and sorrow beneath the changing clouds.

There were songs to sing and hymns to hum that holy night. "Don't be afraid," the clouds sang to me. I began singing Dad's favorite Christmas hymn. *Silent Night! Holy Night! All is calm. All is bright.* We were singing Christmas hymns on a cool, mid-August night. The clouds floated over us transforming into piercing indigo colors.

Somewhere in the timeless night, I heard the sound of rushing water and a rustling of leaves. The wind whispered with the taped music. The sounds of chanting crossed the room. As we sat and listened, the tolling of bells began. At that moment, Dad gasped. His throat fluttered and then he was still. Mother bent over Dad to close his mouth. The bells continued to toll through the vanishing night.

Wisps of clouds descended from the sky. They shrouded the room in a mist of shifting light. In my mind's eye, I saw Dad running far above the house. He sprinted over the fields through the hills. His head was thrown back as he strode through the sky. He was running like a champion through the coliseum.

As I watched, a cloud gradually took the form of a soaring bird flying high over Dad's grape arbor and orchard. Its wings ignited into shafts of crimson and gold as it stretched along the brilliant eastern sky. Nearby, hidden from view, a mourning dove softly cooed to me. Dad was racing to build heavenly projects. It was my sign from heaven. *The clouds were changing colors. They were passing through the silent night.*

All The Saints

Benita pressed deeply into the gnarled tendons of Rudy's legs, long bony hands kneading the middle-aged man's muscles like tortilla dough. As she rolled and pulled his legs over the table, she felt his nerves jump in her withered, thin hands. Rudy leaned forward eagerly as Benita began telling one of her many stories.

"Then what happened?" asked Rudy.

"After the doctor shot the town pharmacist, he was jailed." She punctuated the word "jailed" by digging stiffly into Rudy's calf. Rudy flinched slightly.

"They jailed the doctor?"

A crooked smile formed across the woman's face. "The sheriff jailed the doctor."

"Did the sheriff let him go?" asked Rudy. He braced himself against the brute force of Benita's hands.

She grinned mischievously. "He had to let the doctor out of jail. The doctor kept pestering him all day for cigarettes."

Rudy laughed heartily holding his lower back as Benita pounded pungent olive oil down his leg. He took one deep breath and then relaxed under the glow of the burning vigil candles. The fragrance spiraled before the grim-faced statues of various Catholic saints on the wall niche.

"It is done!" announced Benita. She spoke the last word by punching Rudy's bulging thigh.

"Doña Benita, you have powerful medicine," said Rudy rising from the wood table. "My doctor told me I needed surgery, but you perform miracles."

"I do not perform miracles. They do," she replied. Benita pointed to the elaborately dressed statues that adorned the niche on the wall. Rudy watched the old woman disappear behind the folded green curtains, which cascaded in long ripples to the floor. Behind the partition were mysterious remedies that defied the laws of medical science. To every suffering patient, not cured by modern medicine, Benita admonished, "There is a higher law."

Heaven's laws had looked favorably upon old Benita. Her ox-like strength in advanced age astounded the learned and uneducated alike. No one knew the exact age of Benita, but it was rumored that she was over one hundred years of age. When Benita emerged through the veiled partition, she solemnly carried the sacred remedy in her hands.

The Healer

"What's this?" asked Rudy staring at the brown bag.

"Now listen," said Benita handing Rudy the brown bag. "This herb is very strong. Before you go to bed, mix some lard into this herb and rub it into your leg."

Rudy nodded attentively and tucked the brown bag into his shirt pocket.

"Do not forget what I said," said Benita wiping her hands on her starched, black apron.

"I never forget what you say," answered Rudy with a smile. Glancing into the kitchen, he pointed at the bare kitchen table. "Doña Benita, you have no Mexican bread!"

A gleam of light shot from Benita's dark eyes. Rudy knew exactly what she needed. Ever since Don Pancho's corner grocery store had been razed, Rudy had brought fresh produce and Mexican bread to old Benita.

"I will bring sweet bread tomorrow," promised Rudy walking down the porch. Even the porch steps howled with their own aches and pains. "I want to hear more about the doctor who shot the pharmacist."

After Rudy left, Benita retreated to her flower-patterned sofa. She felt for the battered cushions before sitting. Benita gazed at her "little saints." Benita's dimly lit living room served as a sanctuary for all who sought refuge in her humble domain. The wood table by the curtains had become the sacrificial altar upon which the penitents cast their many burdens. Those who were healed by her hands brought their children and their grandchildren.

Benita knew her divine vocation. As a young woman she had learned the craft well enough to support her family. Medical specialists and doctors could not compete with her intuitive skill to diagnose most medical maladies. With her thin hands, she felt for heart problems, gallstones, stomach disorders, and nerve pain. Her hands had become her eyes. With her hands, she saw beyond the normal constraints of the physical senses. In an age when others yielded to modern medical interventions, Benita's life conformed to the higher, universal laws of nature. No surgeon's knife or prescription drug ever touched her body. The torment and pain of sickness and frailty were foreign to her.

A curtain of darkness dropped over her eyes. "How much time do I have left?" she cried addressing the glass-eyed statues on the wall niche. "Bring me back my granddaughter before it is too late." During times of adversity she petitioned her "saints," and her protectors heard her. They heard Doña Benita's lament. She spoke to them as she crocheted and prayed. Since she had dressed them in velvet and satin clothes, they had to listen. For the masseuse, the world had turned into a dizzying blur of geometric forms. Twilight vision dominated her left eye, where she saw images in varying degrees of light. Benita had never imagined outliving her usefulness to others.

Benita had been raised in Lagos de Moreno, Mexico by her maternal grandmother. She had left home when her uncle sent for her. He was a learned scholar and priest in a large parish. The austere priest indulged his spiritual pride in selecting chosen sibling's offspring to educate. Thus, it was by divine intervention that Benita was literate. However, the Mexican Revolution of 1910 had chaotically changed life's ordered events. Brother turned against brother. Families fought each other. The noble men and women who were not sacrificed to the pagan gods of war and violence, began the long trek to the North. They came by foot and by train to the Promise Land.

Tears welled within Benita as she remembered. Her grandmother had been a bastion of strength and courage. When Pancho Villa and the generals rode through the villages and haciendas blazing a trail of havoc, the old Indian woman had defied them. She was undaunted by their threats and guns and her household remained intact. Thus, it had been Benita's legacy to survive against man and nature. Life's events swirled in Benita's mind until they merged with her blurred vision. Widowed, she had outlived two children and lost a granddaughter, who abruptly left home and never returned. The veil parted over her left eye until she distinguished the form of a small man through the open screen door. Squatting near a converted school bus, the dark-skinned man swayed to the salsa music blaring from the bus radio.

Staring at the bus, Benita sighed. The composition of the barrio had dramatically changed. The Mexicans had moved up town and the Salvadorans had settled into their vacant houses. After seventy years, little of the once virginal landscape remained. Cottonwoods and elms intertwined with each other to spread their limbs across the street. During the day, the reverberating sounds of the train on the railroad tracks echoed through her house. The Santa Fe shook the house with a perpetual rumble like the eruption of an ancient volcano.

Only at dusk did the barrio return to its pristine state. At night the train was silent, and the gentle sounds dominated the quiet barrio streets. From the direction of the northward flowing river, Benita could hear nature's soft lullabies. The night music of hooting owls and chirping crickets filtered through her open windows. For old Benita, there were other songs also. In the stillness of a sultry summer night, she could hear her grandmother singing cradlesongs and her uncle reciting his interminable litanies in Spanish.

On Benita's side of the street lights and houses were sparse. The main street had more potholes than pavement, and this singular neglect deterred not only traffic, but also building prospects. Benita's friends, Rudy and Cuca, were not perturbed by the city planners' oversight. They preferred the solitude. Cuca was a blond-hair woman from El Salvador who lived up the street from Benita. She too, had come to the Promise Land with many expectations and illusions. However, the California romance ended when her husband abandoned the family during her third pregnancy. Through the trials of life, Cuca learned to endure and survive.

Many years ago Cuca had consulted a fortuneteller for Benita. According to the fortuneteller, Benita's prodigal granddaughter was in a distant city faraway. However, Benita had no faith in soothsayers. As Benita's eyes closed, her afternoon meditations were interrupted by Cuca's frantic voice calling from the kitchen.

"Doña Benita, where are you? My baby's brains have fallen." Cuca appeared in the living room with her baby pressed to her bosom. The baby wildly kicked his legs. As Benita felt his fragile head with her skilled hands, she saw that indeed his "brains" had collapsed. The baby's head was enlarged.

"Do as I tell you," she ordered. "Under the kitchen sink is a blue pan. Fill it with warm water, and bring me some salt."

Benita searched the top of the infant's head until she touched the indentation. From the size of the protuberance, she ascertained the problem. The infant had struck his head when he fell from his crib. She massaged the top of the infant's head feeling every crease and contour. This baby was destined to survive. Cuca soon returned with the prescribed remedies.

"Go bring me the towels from the bathroom," directed Benita stripping the infant.

Turning the infant upside down, she dipped his head into the water three times. Benita spread several grains of salt over the baby's tongue. Invoking her "saints" she turned the baby over and began slowly massaging his spine in a rhythmic pattern of self-assured strokes. His screaming became an inaudible whimper, and he soon fell asleep on her lap. Benita's discerning hands had once again quelled life's storms.

One late summer afternoon Benita stood in her storeroom fingering her herbs. She could not distinguish the jars and bags of remedies lining the shelves. The dark veil had dropped over her eyes. Days had turned into endless nights. Benita inhaled the sacred substances. The supply of mint was diminishing. A German lady from across town was coming in the evening, and she needed a potent remedy for stomach pain. As she inhaled the mint tea, she regretted not having been sufficiently grateful for the days she saw with blurred vision. She would give the woman the last remains of the bag.

Slowly, Benita moved toward the kitchen. If only she had not been so hard with her granddaughter, she might not have left home.

Benita searched the wall until she touched her protectors. She clutched the bag of mint tea in one hand, while her other hand lingered on the little "saints." Benita reached for the statues. Invoking her grandmother's name, she lifted up the saint for lost children and began to pray the litanies for the deceased. She scolded her saints harshly. Her "saints" should not forsake her now.

Benita labored to rearrange the saints back into their niche. However, they stoutly refused to take their assigned places. Instead they rocked precariously on the edge of the niche while frowning at Benita.

"Don't fall," Benita commanded.

Clutching the mint tea, Benita shoved the saints impatiently against the wall. Benita lamented not having a daughter to carry on the venerated tradition. Exhausted, Benita fell into the embrace of the battered sofa still muttering to her "saints".

Benita was half asleep when she heard the songs explode into the air with countless trills. The songs were gentle and familiar, as welcome as the loving voices of a family who had once lived peacefully in her humble abode. She heard the voices, half chant, and half song. The neighborhood children sang her name to the sounds of skipping ropes.

"*Doña Benita, Doña Benita,*
Lady of the remedies."

As Benita listened to the melodious chant, she finally understood. Children, in nursery rhymes, revealed life's hidden truths. These were her daughters and granddaughters who had finally returned home. They were her legacy multiplied a hundredfold. The saints had heard her prayers. Her legacy of healing had not only been woven into the fabric of barrio life, but of all life. "God blesses fools and children alike," she muttered to herself.

She heard the back door of the kitchen open. It was Rudy. "I brought your sweet bread," he hollered. A loud thump sounded on the table as he unpacked the rolls of Mexican bread. "Doña Benita, come look at your sweet bread." There was no answer.

"Doña Benita. Doña Benita!"

Hurrying into the living room Rudy knelt beside the sofa. The bag of mint tea rested awkwardly in her wrinkled hands. Her gaze penetrated through the window screens into unknown realms.

"Are you all right?" he asked anxiously.

"No más," she said sadly. "No more remedies."

"What's wrong?" asked Rudy touching her shoulder.

"Go to the storeroom and throw everything out," she ordered.

"What are you saying?" protested Rudy. "I can't throw away your medicines."

"No more remedies," replied Benita shaking her finger at him. "No more remedies."

Rudy shook his head. "This is your life's work."

"That's the way life is," murmured Benita closing her eyes. "That . . . is life."

Benita's eyelids fluttered for an instant. She chuckled as she remembered. Finally, she spoke. "Did I ever tell you what remedy I took the doctor when he was in jail?"

"It must have been a very strong remedy," answered Rudy.

Benita nodded. "I took the doctor a big box of *Lucky Strikes*." She chuckled again before her head dropped. Her respiration came gently like an overdue summer rain until she sighed deeply. The bag of mint tea rolled silently onto the floor as she stretched her worn limbs on the sofa. The sudden rumble of the Santa Fe shook the windowpanes of the house with a blast of fury. Then, like the last toll of a village church bell, it faded into the distance with multiple echoes.

As Rudy sorted out the jars and colored vials from the storeroom, he noticed them. He saw them through the partially parted curtains, which billowed with the revolving fan. They were all hiding their faces from him. High on the niche, Benita's "saints" were turned facing the wall.

The Greeter with Many Names

Maria Francisca stood proudly at the front church door every Sunday morning, where she had stood for more years than anyone could remember. She was the greeter at the parish church. No one had ever appointed her to that ministerial task to greet all parishioners as they entered the church. Years ago, Maria Francisca had appointed herself to be the official parish greeter.

Thus, it came to be that Maria Francisca knew the names of more parishioners than any pastor past, present, or future. She had a talent for remembering names and remembering "something interesting," as she said often, about each parishioner.

Maria Francisca was not beyond walking down the aisles of the church, row by row, to greet unsuspecting church members. She greeted everybody, from the widowed parishioner who sat alone to the occasional Sunday visitor in church. Whereas, the pastor of the church waited in the middle of the church concourse to be greeted by parishioners, Maria Francisca waited at the front door to greet every parishioner.

Tall and well-dressed, Maria Francisca was proud of her Indian heritage. Originally from Pecos, she liked to introduce herself by her five names. When she introduced herself to anyone, she began with her baptismal names, followed by a confirmation name, a maiden name and married surname. Sometimes, she threw in a few other names given to her over the trajectory of her eighty-seven years of existence.

Thus, when the unsuspecting parishioner asked her how long she had been in this country, her answer was straight to the point. "I go back centuries." By no means was she exaggerating in her quick response. Maria Francisca had been descended from a full-blooded Indian grandmother in Santa Fe, and her family lineage went back to the early 1500's. However, this former kindergarten teacher had lived most of her married life in California. The Mohave Desert reminded her of her New Mexico roots. Friendly and outgoing, Maria Francisca took the initiative to learn something of interest, as she said, about every person she met.

"*Mi casa es su casa*," she would say to those of us who visited her. "My house is your house."

Having been a landscape artist, she had a talent for absorbing details and rearranging the disordered into proper order. Every drawer and cupboard in her house was in perfect order. Even her garage looked more like a picture gallery than a garage for tools and vehicles. Her small yard was picture perfect, complete with red roses and geraniums.

For years, Maria Francisca had volunteered at the thrift shop overseen by the Brothers of the local Catholic hospital. It was here she mastered placing discarded items and merchandise into proper order. She knew what was junk and what was of true value. It was at this Catholic thrift store, she purchased her most prized treasures. In her living room, adorned with history books and art objects from around the world, Maria Francisca proudly displayed a silver menorah and a polished keyboard. She wasn't Jewish and she didn't know how to play for that matter, but these thrift store items were her trophy collections which engaged everybody upon entering her house.

"If you're not Jewish, why do you keep a menorah?" was the immediate question. The reply was straightforward.

"The Jewish history is interesting!"

Menorah

For Maria Francisca, anything with educational significance or value was interesting. She was sparse with her compliments, but if she "could learn something" of value from anyone, it was interesting. In her desire to always learn something of value, she even hosted a Seder one Passover. The table was set elaborately with herbs and traditional dishes. All the women wore prayer shawls and read the prayers. Maria Francisca presided and gave the blessing. It was all part of a learning quest to enrich oneself by getting to know the culture and history of others. She loved to say, "This is very interesting. I learned something today." The popular California historian of television fame, *Huell Houser*, couldn't have said it better.

An avid reader of history, she collected many volumes of ancient history and of course, books on the Southwest. Often, I found her reading a history book when I visited. She had a thirst for learning historical facts and details about past cultures and civilizations. It was this love for travel and visiting places that led her and me on a pilgrimage to Mexico City.

It was during this pilgrimage to the Basilica of Mexico City that I learned more about her beyond the friendly greeter I knew from church. When I couldn't find a roommate, she offered to share a room with me for the week. We stayed at a secluded monastery, used for educational purposes, which was walking distance from the Basilica. A local priest had offered to lead a group of us for the festivities celebrated in December.

The trip would coincide with the feast day of *The Virgin of Guadalupe* which was celebrated by thousands of pilgrims from all over the world. According to the story, *The Virgin of Guadalupe* had appeared to the newly baptized Indian peasant, named Juan Diego, to establish her church on Tepeyac hill in 1531. It was on the morning of Saturday 9 December 1531 that the Virgin appeared with a request for a shrine. Three days later, she commanded Juan Diego to gather roses into his tilma, as a proof for the Bishop. When Juan Diego opened his tilma for the Bishop, the roses cascaded to the floor leaving the image of the celestial Lady seen at Tepeyac. It has been said that if the Virgin hadn't appeared, the Indians that Cortez conquered, probably would have resisted any assimilation into the Catholic, European Spanish culture.

Her Indian image now adorns every church, fruit stand, and bus throughout the city.

When our group arrived at the airport, we passed through customs. Standing in line, Maria Francisca chatted with everyone about their place of origin and about their business in the capital. She became so engrossed in conversation with all the tourists standing behind us, we almost missed the bus to our destination. Whether we were buying trinkets in the street corners or waiting in line to enter the Basilica, she greeted and talked to everybody. The stories of faith and healing which the pilgrims shared with us were incredible. Maria Francisca couldn't have been a better guide for finding pilgrims who had been healed by the Virgin.

I don't recall sleeping many hours after our bus tours to the pyramids and tourist destinations ended. As night settled over the old adobe monastery, she and I would slip away out the courtyard, to join the singing pilgrims milling around the Basilica until the dawn hours. On one night six of us crowded into a bug-sized taxi, all piled on top of each other, to see the sights of Mexico City. As I sat on top of Maria Francisca, I anxiously inquired, "Do you mind?"

She blithely replied, "Not at all. This is interesting."

Maria Francisca was a true believer. As we stood together on the last day of our pilgrimage, before the famous tilma of the Virgin, she whispered, "*Our Lady* is here to heal us."

Although, not given to collecting statues or religious objects, she remained strong until the end of her hospice days. For those of us who knew her, we were welcomed both at church and at her home. Whether it was a cup of tea or some historical fact she shared, Maria Francisca shared what she had to offer with everyone. No one was ever turned away. "*Mi casa es su casa*. My house is your house." This was the old California way of the open door, pride in native traditions, and love for the land for its healing blessings. Maria Francisca was a greeter of many names.

Printed in the United States
By Bookmasters